A Transfer of Grace
Island Lives

Copyright (c) 2024

All rights reserved

No part of this book may be used
or reproduced in any manner whatsoever
without the written permission of its author,
except in the case of reviews or
embodied in critical articles.

The right of the writers and artists to be recognised
as the authors of this work has been
asserted in terms of Section 77
of the Copyright, Designs and Patents Act 1988

Published by Western Isles Association For Mental Health

This book was first published in October 2024

This book is sold subject to the condition
that it shall not by way of trade or otherwise,
be lent, resold, hired out or otherwise circulated
without the author's prior consent in any form
of binding or cover other than that in
which it is published and without a
similar condition including this condition
being imposed on the subsequent
purchaser.

Cover image - Linda MacLeod

This book is dedicated to the memory of Donna Keenan -
a much loved and valued member
of Catch 23's Writing Group

Contents

Foreword

Peter Urpeth - 6

Writers

Isabelle Moss - 9
Billie Bambridge - 13
Cathy MacLeod - 19
Mike Dawson - 24
David MacLeod - 27
Shell Bromley - 33
Josie Mansfield Townsend - 39
Bev Poole - 51
Anne Christina Nicolson - 55
Aaron Watt - 59
Rebecca Mahony - 63
Hazel Mansfield - 67
Chris Matheson - 75
Spencer Woodcock - 77
Hilary Sludden - 85
Urszula Ghee Wieckowska - 93
Ozrik Carter - 103

Illustrators

Chris Matheson - 8, 28, 74
Linda MacLeod - 12
Rebecca Mahony - 20
Anne Christina Nicolson - 32
Mark Adams - 40
Josie Mansfield Townsend 48,
Evie Crocker - 50
Keilidh MacKay & Stewart Keith - 54
Hilary Sludden - 60
Zoe Digges - 62, 102
Hazel Mansfield - 68
Janine MacDonald - 78
Aaron Watt - 86
Urszula Ghee Wieckowska 92, 96

Foreword

by Peter Urpeth

Sometimes a line just sticks in your head. It captures a sentiment, a moment in time, the essence of a place, or provokes a memory. Sometimes, its power resonates within and stays with you.

The title of this collection was one such line for me. It captures the warmth of the community in which this work was produced, and its intention to communicate with candour, empathy, and insight. It is a gift from its creators to each other and to the wider world.

In April 2024, I started working with the long-standing and thriving writer's group at Catch 23 - a support service for adults with mental health issues run by Western Isles Association for Mental Health, (WIAMH), a local charity. We quickly fixed on a theme for our project - island life - which would give us the contents of a publication, this publication. The theme was intentionally broad and open to interpretation. It would leave writers the space to define their own response in whichever way they chose.

We held several writing sessions over the next few months, and these became for me some of the most engaging sessions I have ever led. We would spend the first part of the sessions writing, often to prompts I'd bring fresh to each session. Then, after lunch, some time would be spent reading our work for each other. We read in the round, with no critiques allowed. Just listening. Just reading, a communal experience of the joy and power, and, perhaps, the empowerment of storytelling in all its diverse forms.

The works read were often met with laughter at a humorous twist. Sometimes they were met with silence at a moment of profound connection or insight, sometimes sorrow and a supportive word. Reading out loud, being read to bonds a community. I was struck throughout these weeks by the resilience of all those involved. I was struck by their commitment to the simple but powerful act of addressing the blank page, as writers and as artists, with personal thoughts.

Behind the unassuming door of the modest former town house that houses Catch 23 at the edge of the centre of Stornoway, beats the heart of a true and vital community. The term 'oasis' is perhaps over-used, but this is one veritable oasis worthy of the name.

Catch 23 is a place of nourishment, recovery, discovery, creativity. Every day, meals are cooked and shared in a warm and buzzing kitchen. In a front room, and in an outhouse at the rear of the building now converted to an arts studio, the magic of creative endeavour is encouraged and shared.

Such shared communal action is therapeutic for sure. It is supportive, a unique salve against the loneliness and isolation that the experience of poor mental health can bring to any or all of us.

But this is also a place of great strength and courage. A place of mutual nurturing. That is what I found there. This work it is a gift, and an invitation to connection. A sharing of insight and truth. A connection that is truly a transfer of grace.

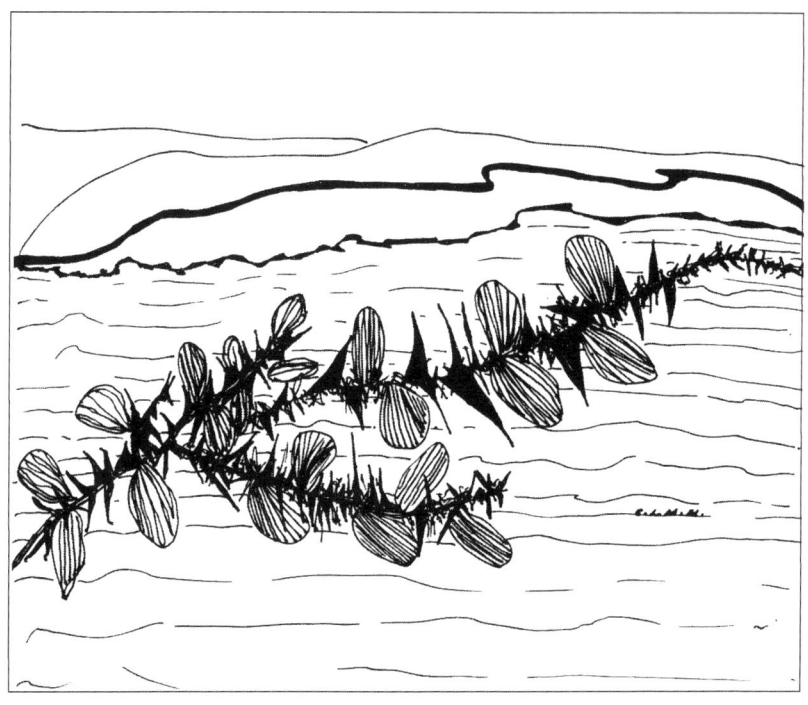

Artist: Chris Matheson for Isabelle Moss's 'Flowering'

Isabelle Moss

Flowering

The bursting yellow, spring flowering of gorse
draws the light to the burnt road,
curving around the stretched-out bay,
below the bright, pale blue of the sky,
hills flattened, pours the gifting ocean

New beginnings, you said,
but the freshness requires old endings,
will you be strong enough?
Hold the entwining memories back?
Rhythms of life sliding forward

So, as I watch waves that lap
the gentle curve of the smooth inlet,
I glance towards the myriad blue horizon,
hope in the heart, tears in the eyes,
for the opening of my world.

Friends

Power from shore to shore,
the crested waves that shape,
pound, the home, flung of the
Hebridean Islands

Fused by the drenching rain,
tentacles of traditions, the holding on,
thrusting a new order,
the mix a work in progress

Who, what have you grown?
Others carry their yesterdays,
to your patchwork world,
the sum island creation

And so, the rhythms of my being,
jagged journey to fit in,
the friends that emerge
from the shifting sea shoreline

Rattles our pebbles together,
the drawback, ebb and flow,
made, the connection,
on the sun burnt golden sands.

In the Silence

Love your silence,
when the memories
of your rain-stained
thoughts settle

Ideas that the sun baked
heat hushed,
re-emerging in the still
quiet of the falling cloak

Of blue to the horizon,
from the silent sky,
passing, pouring of traffic
on hold, paused existence

Words that unravel,
knots in existence,
Tumbling in the silence,
Rebuilds the mind.

Artist: Linda MacLeod for Billie Bambridge's 'Bosta Beach'

Billie Bambridge

Bosta Beach, Berneray, Isle of Lewis

A rollercoaster of a single-track road through a rocky outcrop leads me down to a small, wall-enclosed, cemetery. The weather worn antique stone graves adorned with feathery lichens and dried moss intermingled with later shiny black marble headstones. Some were now sadly forgotten. Some lovingly tended.

A small iron-age settlement nestled behind the graveyard is a perfect backdrop and draws me along the narrow path. The thick luscious machair generously studded with wild meadow flowers is soft and springy underfoot. The air was sweet. The breeze gentle.

Turning back the way I had come, the view of the beach below is heartbreakingly beautiful and I draw a breath. Walking down through sandy dunes, the black-faced, curly horned sheep are grazing, undisturbed by my presence.

The two resident Highland cows are warily watching. One ebony black, one patchy shades of brown. Their beefy bodies belying their beautiful faces. Deep knowing eyes battling dark lashes. Peering out at me through long thick fringes, their horns sitting proudly upright above shaggy hair.

Trying not to make eye contact, I pick my way down towards the beach and the white sandy shore.

The sea is all shades of turquoise on the horizon but perfectly crystal clear as it softly laps at the shoreline, gently tumbling the tiny pebbles, the fine sand damp, my bare feet leaving footprints as I walk. My pale pink toenails almost shell like in the morning light.

A decaying sheep's carcass rotting on a rocky ledge. A washed-up seal pup its bones bleached white.

Oystercatchers all walking in line. Their red stockinged long legs stretching out in front of them, their long-stepped walk making me smile. Like line dancers, their matching slim red bills dipping down low into the wet sand as they stride along the shoreline looking for tasty morsels, each ready to dine of the fruits the sea has left for them. Only their small scratchy bird prints left in their wake, a thin trailing line on the shore broken only by garlands of seaweed.

The sound of the lapping ocean washing the pale sand clean. The song of the Oystercatcher stridently calling. Gulls silently swooping overhead. A white-tailed eagle soaring high.

The changing light as the day passes. Early morning dawn eventually welcoming evening dusk. The moon silvery, mirroring its shimmering glow on the darkening sea as the tide slowly creeps forward. My footprints magically disappearing. All traces of the day quietly washed away.

The heavy iron Time and Tide bell hauntingly, eerily ringing out across the silhouetted moonlit bay.

The sky was now a faded purple velvet above the blackening water. The many stars glinting through the twilight. A sense of peace and wellbeing enfolding me.

The Road To Nowhere

Crystal stood on the Bridge to Nowhere, her hair zigzagging across her face in the light breeze. She had spent the last evening after Summer Solstice watching a stunning sunset slip down behind the Callanish Stones, and patiently waited through the twilight for the full moon to rise above the mountain.

Now this morning she had come to her special place to walk on the beach below, among the towering sea stacks that still left her in awe. How life had worn away at them, leaving them battered and scarred yet still beautiful and enduring.

This was her island. She had come here alone a decade ago and now she was a solitary figure on the bridge, her skirt billowing in the breeze.

As she stood staring out at the horizon, she let her mind wander, remembering what had brought her here to Lewis. Her mum Angela, known as Angel, would have loved it here. Thoughts of her mum brought a smile to her lips.

Angel had been a child of the sixties. A free spirit, young and carefree, reckless. Running wild in long flowing skirts and jangling silver bangles. Bringing a breath of life and joy into Crystal's bland, stifling world.

Crystal's home life with her father was so very different, so conventional. He was so strict with her, forever telling her she was just like her mother, and would make nothing of herself - she was heading on a road to nowhere. He was so very bitter, but Crystal knew deep down that he had never really stopped loving her mother.

Angel would randomly gate-crash into their lives and then swoop out again, often leaving chaos and confusion behind her. Crystal was always so happy and excited to see her. They would laugh and hug and do crazy spontaneous things together while her father would scowl in the background. And then, just when Angel was used to her mother being in her life again, Angel would kiss her daughter goodbye, promising she would soon be back. Angel's promises were seldom kept. Birthdays and Christmases would come and go with no word. But then, Angel would appear out of the blue and Crystal's world would come alive again for the few short days or weeks Angel stayed around.

Eventually, her father married a woman much like himself. She was good for him and he became a little less hard on Angel when she did sporadically turn up. A little less judgemental, a little kinder. Angel wasn't aging well. A combination of White Horse whiskey and life on the road helping her to lose her once youthful bloom. Her colourful flowing clothes were now a little faded, her silver bangles a little tarnished. Looking slightly more jaded each time she re-appeared.

As Crystal worked her way through school, her father just got stricter with her, often muttering that she would end up just like her mother, and fairly had a fit when she tentatively suggested she would like to go to art college. So Crystal dutifully left school and went to work with one of the local estate agents.

She got on well and found she enjoyed trying to match tenants to suitable homes. She soon started saving for a deposit herself. She could no longer live with her father, being more disapproving of her than ever. Everything she did seemed to annoy him: the clothes she wore, the boys she dated.

Angel was turning up a little more often as the years passed and Crystal was secretly hoping that once she had her own place, her mum would visit more regularly. Maybe settle down and stay awhile. Get herself straight. Crystal would gently suggest this several times, but Angel would always smile vaguely and say maybe. The smell of malt on her breath, her once slim body now too thin, her flowing dress now drowning her.

There were only a handful of mourners at her mother's funeral, no-one knowing where or how to contact any friends she may have had. After the wicker coffin had been lowered into the ground, Crystal took refuge in her little flat, where she had nursed Angel for the last few weeks of her life.

Her father's continuous belittling of both Angel and herself during that time was so hurtful. Crowing that, Angel had only herself to blame and her daughter would end up the same way with her floaty dresses and motorbike riding boyfriend. Like mother, like daughter.

She was at work typing up new property lettings when she saw the croft to let along with a small cottage. It was on the Island of Lewis, somewhere she had never been, never having travelled further north than Dundee. But she fell in love with the idea, some of her mother's spirit forging her on.

Within weeks, she had given in both her notice at work and on her flat and had started packing up her life into boxes. Her clothes, books, small bits and pieces she had bought to make the flat homely. Pottery lamps and vases, cosy throws, and cushions, trailing houseplants. She carefully packed it all into her little hatchback.

The last words her father spoke to her were harsh and hurtful. How he had always known she would end up just like her mother? On a road to nowhere, he repeated to her yet again, his own personal mantra.

She had driven away, never looking back, having no reason to return.

Crystal stood on the Bridge to Nowhere and looked back as she heard distant giggling. Her two young daughters chasing up the Road to Nowhere, their father trailing behind them, laughing as they all made their way up to the bridge.

They would share a picnic on the beach and then go home to their little cottage and croft they had managed to purchase a few years earlier. It was hard work, but she loved the life she had made here. Her home, her work, her family, the life they all shared.

Crystal waved and running down to meet them, knelt and hugged her daughters to her.

Yes, she was on The Road to Nowhere and there was nowhere else she would rather be.

Cathy MacLeod

Granny Mac and The Boy - Lewis Castle Grounds

Boy and I
took a walk today,
under a grey sky,
we sparkled along the track,
(he chose the right hand path),
when I let go
he skipped and ran ahead
as I guided him from behind,
leaning on my staff, my stick,
navigating the muddy puddle,
we got dirty shoes,
but it didn't get to us,
it didn't matter,
in the very great scheme of things

Looking on the abandoned house,
he said it creeped him out,
even though flowers grew
in the over run garden,
so we back-tracked and took
another path into the woods,
there we met Draggie Moss Doran,

Artist: Rebecca Mahony for Cathy Macleod's 'Granny Mac and The Boy - Lewis Castle Grounds'

the tree dragon,
too wet to fly on today,
so we stroked him and told him
we loved him, and we'd see him again
in the summer

We went as far as the glade,
the circle of worshipping trees,
we spun about and retraced our steps,
opening the ancient gates
Boy said ancient was a curse,
I laughed and said,
no, ancient is only antique,
oh, he said, satisfied,
thoughts of Egyptian curses leaving his mind

We held hands and made it across the main road,
avoiding a big wet puddle,
in front of us, huge on the hill,
stood the monument - a memorial of war,
we agreed war should stop
and that the monument looked like a huge chess piece,
he said he would learn chess one day,
and that he and I were the white pieces,
peace, I think he's learning already!

Then after the 30 mph sign we were home.
I let go his hand and he managed to open
the door all by himself

We were home, my home,
his second home-from-home

He sat on his chair,
this is how cool people sit Granny,
he smiled and he switched on the telly.

Catching Mackerel with Lion Beag & Raco
(Uig 2010)

Moon yellow boat
coming to grips
with the ongoing waves,
ripping tiger stripes
from the bloom of the depths,
quicksilver slaps the black tarred wood,
the transformation in colour
seems a sure sign of the right to harvest,
we are blessed,
through the trials of man,
with luck and ancient knowledge,
we are blessed,
by the hook
by the line
by the depths
by the boat
by our company
by wisdom
by favour
by the great mystery,
we eat well that night and the next day,
appetites nourished and provided for,
this then, is the blessing
fulfilled.

Mike Dawson

Eilean an Fraoich Haiku Cycle

Hùisinis

A dying sperm whale's eye
watches five hundred pairs of ravens
dance around a hilltop.

Toddun

Two male golden eagles
spin talon to talon, claw to claw,
their queen circles in the air around them.

Loch an Eilean

A raven plunges deiseal, spinning
black snowflake caught by the wind,
black throated diver cok-coks a welcome.

Loch an Tairbeairt

An eagle soars the wind
as I fish the lonely loch,
we both watch and hunt.

Bun Abhainn Eadarra

A pod of porpoises
weave a bubblenet
to catch their mackerel.

Time and Tide

Time and tide wait for no-one
we adapt to them,
night and day roll past for all
and hold us as thralls

Time and tide wait for no-one
the waves hit the beach
trying to teach
that time and tide
wait for no-one

The waves' bright foam
calls us home
time and tide wait for no-one.

David MacLeod

I love Lewis

Pearlescent pools across the moor,
with such a sight I'm never poor,
from up upon a pearl grey sky,
the raindrops fall to please the eye

To form a landscape, pattern of lochs,
and mountains high to please us jocks,
wear solid wellies, with thick socks,
and let's embark upon a walk

'Cross heathered hills, unfettered sheep,
heading for the highest peak,
through old peat bogs, seldom a slog,
run rivers green, a shiny scene

New trees abound, set your mind sound,
fresh breeze disperses any cloud,
to be a native of this land,
full of colour makes me proud,
span the sky, with Lewis eyes,
a sight to draw a heartfelt sigh

One of joy, no sign of sorrow,
I will come again tomorrow,
the view will change with season's end,
yet I'll be back here once again

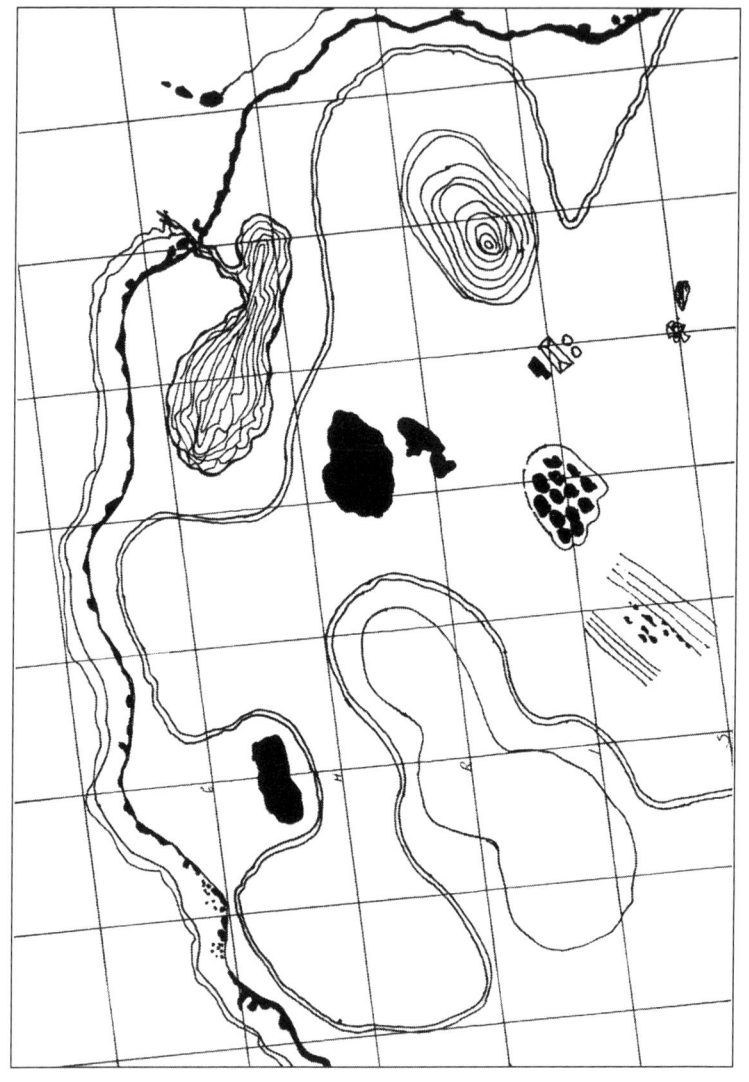

Artist: Chris Matheson for David MacLeod's 'I Love Lewis'

To see a land so different still,
yet sunk in wonder my heart fills,
snow laid deep upon the ground,
warmth of view thaws any chill

Expanse of space on golden beaches,
hues my face, colour of peaches,
wondrous tides roll in and go,
set my mind to a peaceful flow.

Stock Up

Up hill, down dale, all gather round, come hear my tale,
'tis one to tell and at its end, it's one to all I will reveal,
come be intrigued, of wise words heed,
another tale you won't believe

It starts off well with clear intent,
but goes downhill, to my lament...

Woke up one morn, my heart intent,
on gaining needed nourishment,
there was no milk for cereal,
ranted and raged till I grew ill

Twenty six miles the nearest shop,
I set my mood to further drop,
twenty six miles it seems so far,
just as well I have a car

Through winding roads, I boldly go,
need breakfast just to start the show,
to top it all, I'll have you know,
it only starts to bloody snow

Twenty six miles of trepidation,
I roll up to the destination,
walk up to the counter top,
wipe away my own sweat flop,
a pint of milk my dear I say,

she looks at me with some dismay,
we have none sir, I'm sad to say,
the ferry did not sail today

It seems it broke down in the night,
so could not bring much needed freight,
it will not sail until the 'morrow,
we will phone and let you then know

Nothing for me, home I must go,
and here endeth my tale of sorrow.

Artist: Anne Christina Nicolson for Shell Bromley's 'Surface Rock'

Shell Bromley

Surface Rock

The past here is close to the surface and, sometimes, is sinking back into it. Empty houses fall apart in the middle of villages, missing roofs, windows, doors, walls. They look as though they should carry ghost stories, as though they should be in a film about an abandoned world. Except, right next door, is a family home. That house is abandoned, but the place itself is not.

Blackhouse ruins sit in gardens, and the footprints of cleared villages have left imprints in the peats. The present has always built upon the past. But here it more often builds just a bit to the side, leaving still-visible the traces of what was - the ongoing making and unmaking of homes clearer to the eye.

Then there's the family history. Everywhere has it. Back in Lincolnshire, I knew someone was angered, to the point of feeling betrayed, because a twin moved one town over. That twenty-minute drive may as well have been a sea as far as she was concerned, her hometown an island nation. They were natives and were meant to stay there. I was an outsider with different vowels, despite being born one county over.

My mother and her siblings grew up in that county in a town most of them were born in, and one still lives there. I used to feel that was more home than where I lived, because my mum knew so many people, and my grandma knew everyone else. But I didn't grow up there. The best I did was visit.

The day of Grandma's funeral, I arrived early and walked around key places one more time, saying goodbye. I haven't been back since. The connection was through Grandma, not something between the town and me.

I can't trace my family back far. Grandma cut off all contact with, and knowledge of, her father for reasons never fully revealed, but disturbingly hinted at.

My mum cut off contact with her dad for very clearly stated reasons, to the point I often forgot that grandad existed. I watched him go into the ground, the only grandparent to have a straight-up burial in a church graveyard. His coffin seemed a prop, and the churchyard a set.

I felt nothing.

After, at the wake, mum, and my aunt and uncles shared stories of days out in the village where he was buried, a short way from the town they grew up in. It was fitting, they agreed, that grandad be buried in a place so significant to them all. I'd never heard the name of the place before that day, had never heard it talked about.

At talks here on Lewis, people put their hands up to tell the visiting expert on Norse place names all about the great-great-aunt who lived in their place, the earlier ancestor who lived on the other coast. It's hardly everyone, of course, it isn't, but it feels that more of that is visible here. A greater percentage of those living here have those memories and connections at hand. Just as so much rock pokes up through the earth. The scraping of the surface is thinner, the underneath barely neath at all, and it's old rock, some of the oldest surface rock in the world. That rock predates all of humanity, most of the mountains elsewhere on earth, and everyone's history. However much people remember, however long their family has lived here, it's only from a human perspective that it's been a long time.

I comfort myself that, to the rock, we are all newcomers.

Thought

'I thought you'd be able to see all the way around,' mum says.

She turns in a bemused circle on the path, as though expecting the Atlantic to wash into view from the east coast of Lewis.

It's not the first time someone has assumed an inaccuracy about this island I now live on, but it is one of the more surprising. It's a stick-in-the-mind-like-a-splinter one, the sort that pricks and bothers you more than its size should dictate.

'How small have you being picturing it as?' I ask, images of a cartoon mound of sand with a couple of coconut trees flashing through my mind.

That stumps her.

With a sheepish grin, she turns back to me.

'I suppose you did tell me there were two supermarkets. I don't know where I thought they'd fit.'

We move on, mum throwing the bit of heather my youngest dog brought her, and me wondering where all the other things I'd told her about had wandered off to in her mind - the arts centre, the leisure centre with its pool, the Catch 23 drop-in place. All the villages. The entire stone circle. I know I've spoken about the castle and its grounds, that I've waxed lyrical about several beaches and said how long it's taken to reach them.

'Did you really think you'd be able to stand at the end of my village and see all around the whole island?' I ask, as we reach the far point of the path.

We giggle at that, but I still find it poking at my brain, that misconception of hers, for the rest of the walk and beyond.

When I got here, I was surprised by the lack of clear paths on walks, having cut my metaphorical teeth and blistered my literal feet on Lakeland trails. There's less expectation there that you'll divine your way across a patch of unmarked land that's halfway to water. That difference took some getting used to. Mum hasn't seemed to notice.

I was intrigued by the ruins of blackhouses in gardens, by the half-shells of old houses rooted beside new ones. I was intrigued by what I assumed to be an attempt to start a thriving agricultural industry by burying cars. At the end of the street where I grew up, a brand-new car sat on a lawn until it fell apart. The girl it had been bought for never passed her test. It was an oddity. A waste. Eventually, the engine fell right out onto the grass. I'm reminded of it often since moving to Lewis, where I've seen a caravan fetched up against the wall of a ruined house. I've wandered past a car rusting at the side of a beach and realised I'm standing on top of a piece (at least) of a part-buried car in my garden. When that one sprouts, I'll be able to have a freshly picked car.

If Mum's mental image were correct, there'd be no need for cars on the island, because you'd be able to walk the whole thing round.

The Clisham

Being one with the land
is all well and good,
until the peat swallows you,
up to the knees.

Josie Mansfield Townsend

The Rock

I am the rock that sits outside your door,
I'm mysterious,
an unknown species,
dark grey in shade
I think I've existed for an aeon or more,
I'll still be here when your memories fade

At night I delight in tripping you up,
it's not my fault I blend in with the dark,
in the day I'm relied upon as a seat or crutch,
or a marker for the edge when parking up

I am the boulder that has watched you grow older,
when you split your knee falling off your bike,
when you were upset and needed a place to hide,
when you went for a hike and needed respite,
I comforted you, a monolith of calm to your plight

I am the stone that holds all the secrets
from the man's field to the town's end,
and everything in between,
you wouldn't believe
the things I've seen

Artist: Mark Adams for Josie Mansfield Townsend's 'The Rock'

I'll keep them, trust
till I fade into dust

That's me, the ancient landmark,
who will always be there,
and never hesitate
to trip you in the dark.

A Letter to the Moor

Dear Moor,

How are you? It's been a while since we've hung out.

I've been thinking about some of the times we've had, and I miss them. I don't think I ever thanked you for keeping me company.

Do you recall how I would run to you every time I was upset? I'd lay on your peat banks, moss-aged stones, or on the drier parts of your little valleys. I would cry about the latest woe, nestled amongst your wild grasses. You whispered to me, brushing the hair from my tear-stricken face, comforting me with your presence. I knew you would always listen.

Sometimes I would be there all day. The skies would darken, and I, once a bright silhouette on your heathery landscape, blended into the shadows. "I'll fade into this moor." I thought. I'd live as a wild person, exist off of the ends of grass and sweet honeysuckle. I'd befriend the sheep for company, and weave a blanket out of their discarded wool. I'd make a pillow of bog cotton, and a slingshot out of those plants with the round brown heads. The bugs would learn to respect me as their leader and warn me of potential threats like cows, rainstorms, bears, and parents on the warpath.

Oh, I remember being invaded by one such bug in these moments. I would leap up and dance about. Yelling at it to get off and stop this betrayal at once. Maybe I wasn't the Leader type. Without fail, I would say my farewells and rush back to the haven of warm food, hugs, and beings that could talk. Beings that were all too unaware of my Grand Plans. Maybe tomorrow, I'd say to myself.

It really has been too long. I'll try to visit soon, my friend. Thank you for everything.

Forever Yours,

Josie.

Moments of Silence

Silence stretches time,
it coats the air with expectation,
breaths caught in throats
to uphold the moment

Silence is a stage
for the birds to sing and the grass to whisper,
for the mind to wander to distant realms,
unrestrained by distractions

Silence teaches composure,
the self-control and confidence,
to step lightly on the ice of the frozen moment,
embracing the balance painted by quiet

Silence is the eye of the storm,
an island surrounded by fire,
it's beautiful, from this haven of absence,
calm in the knowledge, it will sink into flames

Silence is the gap on the page,
the room reserved for hopeful innovation,
and an opportunity of creation,
a prerequisite for the birth of sound,
and everything seen all around

Silence is my faithful companion,
who's always there at the end of all sentences,

it holds me tight in its arms,
as I drift off to sleep in the night

Silence is a guide,
it walks with me in dreams,
one day it will take me to the afterlife,
where we'll reside together for all eternity.

The Sounds I Miss

I miss the sound of the table saw
whirring late into the dark,
it meant we were progressing,
and it made my heart restart

I miss the sound of the wheezing cough
that accompanied my dad,
I knew that he was near to me,
but I always felt so bad

I miss the sound of the coal bucket
we used to fuel our fire,
warmth we made to spite the rain,
at the cost of dry attire

I miss the sound of frustration
as my older siblings played,
a daring escape from boredom
I was allowed to watch not make

I miss the sound of the howling wind
that seeped through gaps in the wall,
knowing I was tucked up safe
when I was very small

I miss the sound of the roaring waves
that crashed upon the rocks,
freedom to be loud outside,
a time that seems to be lost

I miss the sound of thunder
that painted candlelit rooms,
marshmallow fuelled companions
awaiting power-cut news

I miss the sound of being alive
in the childhood left behind.

Artist: Josie Mansfield Townsend for her own 'Storm Kathleen - Tantrum Queen'

Storm Kathleen - Tantrum Queen

It's been very windy this week on the island. Storm Kathleen seems to be responsible. It grounded my flight home from a rare excursion to Glasgow. I was permitted to return the next day.

So that's the news, now onto the olds: my father. Yes, this is one of those reflections on a passed family member.

My dad always claimed he was as old as the wind. I believe he was trying to immortalise himself. Spoilers - it worked. For me, at least. Yet he requested that when he did inevitably pop off, he'd like to be put on a boat and pushed out to sea. Of course, that's a tad illegal. So, when we finally get the tombstone sorted out, maybe we'll get a little boat inscribed on it. Then people can think he was a sailor, a fisherman, a local.

In my mind, he's free to be what I like, so I made him into the wind itself. He can push the sails of his own ship and drift off to new horizons.

He always did like to forge his own path, and the thing about wind is, it's always there. Cheekily tipping over your bins, tousling your hair, and extending your holidays.

On a final note, my sister is called Kathleen. It looks like things got a bit muddled and my dad is now is named after her. So that's Storm Kathleen, or, in other words, my dad, the Tantrum Queen.

Artist: Evie Crocker for Bev Poole's 'My Island'

Bev Poole

My Island

Upon arriving on the ferry in 2000, I was overwhelmed by the beauty of the islands: golden beaches, turquoise seas, colorful wild flowers, and heather-covered moors. Also, the wildlife on land, in the air, and at sea.

The local people were welcoming, with a gentle accent. Some days the wind can be heard whistling around the chimney pots as it spreads the warm smell of the peat fires. My favourite sound, though, is the gentle, haunting sound of the Gaelic psalm singing escaping from the many churches.

Sadly, for me, though, this beautiful island has always been seen through the haze of mental illness. For myself, whose life is plagued with this curse, there is a place of refuge, Catch 23, a second home, a place of safety and friendship. It lies behind a burgundy door, rugged in appearance.

Many pass by without seeing it, and for some, it may be misunderstood. I find it a place that welcomes me with open arms. Its staff offer a listening ear, a warm smile, and a hug if wanted. Those places in my brain that have been ravaged by depression and psychosis have found peace, restoration, and hope within its walls.

When I cannot find the strength to cook, I am offered a healthy meal. Through its many groups, I have found within myself an artist and a writer.

It is the one place on the island that has supported me for so many years, good days and bad. Without the support of Catch 23, my path would have been so much more difficult to tread.

Silence

A busy day in Stornoway. The sounds enter my ears, but also invade through my pores.

It vibrates as if carried by my blood until it fills every organ. The pressure is building in my brain; it is scrambling any sense of peace and calm.

All I want is a few moments of silence to find my peaceful soul.

As I leave behind the busy streets, over the wooden bridge, I hear the gentle stream travelling to the harbour and a few ducks calling to be fed. A sense of relief takes over as the sound of traffic is absorbed by the rock wall and the overhanging green trees.

Progressing down the well-trodden path, the quiet footsteps and smiles of others soothe me. As I look upwards, I see the castle standing proud, timeless, holding within its walls the memories of past generations.

Turning around, I see the freshly cut green lawns and the pink rhododendrons.

Their perfume envelops me. All I hear now is the sweet birdsong. With this quiet comes calmness, a sense of being one with nature.

Artists: Keilidh MacKay & Stewart Keith for Anne Christina Nicolson's 'Now Go Pick Up Every Leaf'

Anne Christina Nicolson

Now Go Pick Up Every Leaf

The gossip (as everyone else sees it) -
like a virus, it grows,
spawning mercilessly,
like an evolutionary monster,
creating copies, not quite like itself,
sometimes on one side,
sometimes on the other,
tearing apart friends and families,
telling lies

The gossip (how it sees itself) -
like a tree it grows,
naturally reproducing,
beautifully creating new life,
sometimes on the other side,
sometimes on one,
separating those who should be parted,
speaking politics.

The Taigh Ceilidh

It was a place of stones
then a place of rock,
then it was a place of stones again,
during Covid.
Now it is the Taigh Ceilidh,
a bookcase for Gaelic books,
and Gaelic scrabble above
windows and art work,
solid table and, well
I don't honestly remember,
what chairs as I bring my own
wherever I go

There's a friendly welcome
from whoever's serving,
I do remember the steepness of the stairs,
fortunately, only two,
the most I can manage going up

It's nice to hear Gaelic spoken,
though I don't speak it myself,
I can just about order in Gaelic
with help from the phonetic how-to-order board,
but more than that and I struggle.

Stuck On You

I loved the island
long before I became stuck on it,
as I loved my house,
long before I became stuck in it

I hate the pavements,
my rattler earning its name
with every step,
but I love the streets
with their interesting shops either side

I love my church,
a place for a tea and scones
or, for me, water and biscuits

The places I miss most,
now I am unable to visit,
are the rock pools and moors
with their microcosms
of island and ocean life,
I just would love to
see them again,
even for a fleeting visit.

The Undesirable Residence

His house was in a state that only a single Lewis crofter can get into. Two inches of dust and dirt covered every surface. Blinds and lace curtains that had not been washed since his mother, spouse, or last slave's death. Layers coated and clogged the sinks and toilet. A tear came to his eye (he did not let it drop for fear it might cleanse a surface), as he watched the last one of knick-knacks decaying.

He'd never bothered or understood the need for a clean home–until she'd died. Now the smell of his own urine pervaded his nostrils, disgusting even himself. He'd had no card game in the house since six months after she'd died. He'd stopped asking soon afterwards when the dog seemed unwilling to enter. Fungus was growing round the bottom of the cupboard, an orange finger pointing to him as he'd always imagined she had.

Aaron Watt

Mental Health on a Small Island Called Stornoway

Living on an island,
everybody knows everybody,
they know your business,
they know your family,
but they do not know
the struggles you face
in your mind

The mind can be a dark,
sombre, place,
and being on an island
with no escape
makes it worse

I've been suicidal,
I've lost the will to live,
I've self harmed,
I've hospitalised myself,
and still I struggle

But Catch 23,
and the lovely people within,

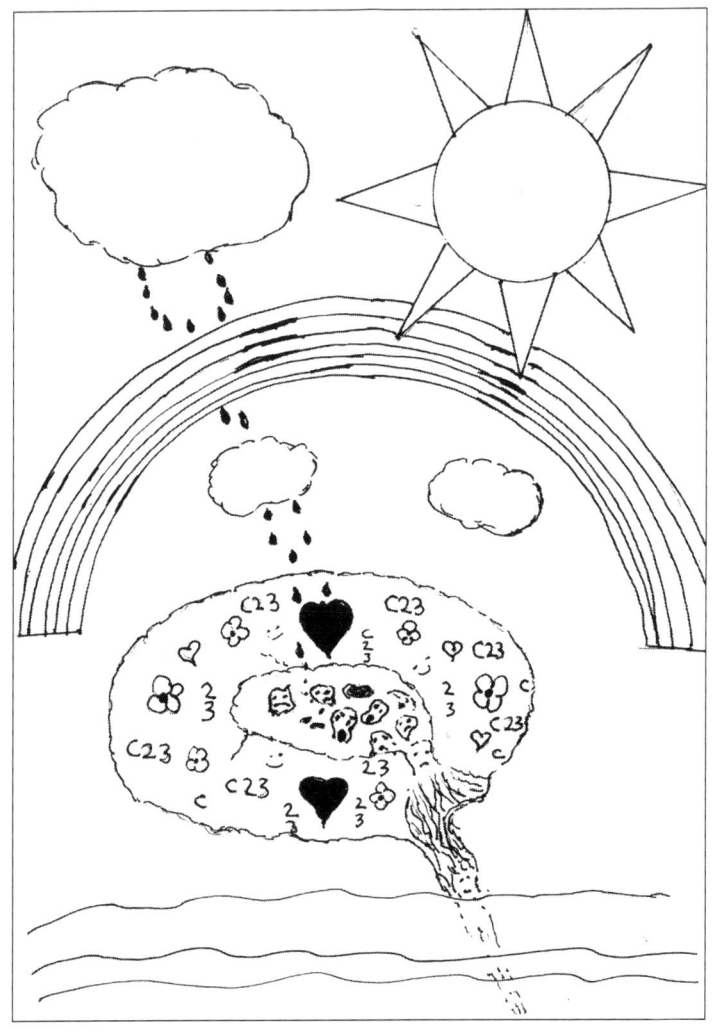

Artist: Hilary Sludden for Aaron Watt's 'Mental Health on a Small Island Called Stornoway'

have saved me and made me realise
there is a light at the end of the tunnel

Rebecca with her understanding,
Keilidh with her loving heart,
Linda with her bright ideas,
Hilary with her hilarious jokes -
maybe island life isn't so bad,
with the undying power
of the Catch 23 family.

Artist: Zoe Digges for Rebecca Mahony's 'Mermaid Moment'

Rebecca Mahony

The Girl from Everywhere and Nowhere

"Where are you from?"
Followed in quick succession by,
"no, where are you really from?"
Are the two questions guaranteed
to make me feel
simultaneously exposed and unseen,
sad, squeamish and uneasy

I don't know how to answer,
with grace, sincerity or simplicity,
without my response eliciting discomfort
or apology from the asker,
my life story, my heritage, my history,
is simply not straightforward

Leicester is my hometown,
where I lived aged 0-18,
Nottingham my chosen place to live aged 18-34,
Slough the place where I was born,
my adoptive parents are from Yorkshire and Lancashire,
my birth mother is Chinese Malaysian,
my birth father is Irish

I was 34 when I landed in Lewis,
and now 52 consider it my adoptive home,

when recently asked where I am from,
by a well-meaning retired minister,
when out for a walk one day,
I point and laugh and say "over there!"

As I age I feel a growing sense of freedom,
and have lost the urge to blend in,
there is strength in being other,
with no ties to bind me,
no roots to connect me,
I am free to just be me

I am free-floating and can choose
where to land,
to put down roots,
to make connections,
to join a tribe,
or not.

Mermaid Moment

Fleetingly at one with the sea,
imagining myself a mermaid,
I turn and swim down
through the mesmerising,
emerald forest of kelp

I glance up through the dancing,
turquoise light of the
sun-kissed Hebridean sea,
in awe, I accidentally inhale
a mouthful of salty seawater

I emerge rapidly
through the cold salt froth,
choking and gulping for air
I am suddenly reminded
of my human frailty.

Home

Home is where the heart is,
So they say,
mine is not native,
but firmly planted
in my adopted island Home
of Lewis

Generally kept busy,
getting on with living
through the common,
wind-battered,
wet and wild days,
and the flat grey dull days

Whilst yearning for
the rare and precious,
halcyon high days,
the gay days, the fine days
the beach days, the gala days

Long buoyant
cloudless days,
full of light,
laughter,
and endless possibilities
stretched optimistically
before us.

Hazel Mansfield

At The Peats in the Late 1990s

Non-fiction data

> Deep in the trenches digging up peats
> like gold, they are squares of heat
> set up on the corners of land, so they are
> ready for the cutting, ready for the fire

Nearly a song

We walked a long way from the mainland, travelling within the tide. We took the lower pathway within democracy and arrived. The lower branch we sat upon, resting among friends, and gifted the rich heartland of the hive.

Digging peats with a irsach (tairsgeir). Cutting turf for fuel, patching, and stitching, and cutting through the grainy well-oiled ground, thick and blanketing the igneous, metamorphic, and sedimentary rock, left lain in the seas by the ages, and just brushing the sky.

Spoken with a wee short blessing, casting our eye to the wind, we tarried hardly a moment as the sharp axe sliced through the peat. Cut and lift, and cut once more. We lifted a bank above the ground and stacked it in the field like straw bales to slow dry in the wind. We tarried a little,

Artist: Hazel Mansfield for her own 'At the Peats in the Late 1990s'

while enough to turn and collect the rich wealth cut by the generations of the wetlands, of the life-rich surface of the aeon-aged gneiss, covering the planet.

Taking in the peats, my friend, is a moment of certain fire. For when the winter's dawn in cold and wind, and the middle of the house is the fire, they'll be songs of these things in a moment's leisure, and I'll speak about carrying the inter-generational slang with the peats to the bank and with the lyre.

Non-fiction data, firsthand spoken

Once, in the past when we first arrived in this little corner of Europe, we were shown how to cut peats by people of the village, from a house rich with children, and of the deep roots of this island. Just put the turf where the last cut was, and lift the cut peat up over the land, and place it flat as far away as the iron will throw. Return some days later and stack four in a square with a single lid on. Then gather the stacks and later, take home.

We co-inherited some peat banks high on the hillside where peats are still cut to this day. We set to with instructions, a home-made cutter, a wheelbarrow, and a lorry, enthusiasm and children.

For a few years all heat in the house came from the peats, cut in the summer, dried and stacked for the future, either this winter or next, and fired in a Rayburn that fed the hot water, the radiators, and the stove.

The savings in money in those years were enough to provide for a household of children, of basics and extras, with parents happy and able through the certainty of fuel.

These are gifts we treasure, and the gifts we found

when first we arrived in this land, in this little land holding up a corner of Europe.

The heart of the home is the fire.

Community

In the outer Hebrides, the heart of the community is the Clo Mor, the Harris Tweed.

Here in the Outer Hebrides, where the Harris Tweed gathers the community, the heart of the Clo Mor is the gather (Fank Feis), where they waulk the Tweed.

I started using Harris Tweed because it is beautiful, and the simple weave and texture suits skill transfers. I make a few Stitch-It-Yourself Harris Tweed multi-kits for one or more, providing everything needed to make it, including a pocket, two lapels, and a heart pomander, with pattern, pin, needle, and thread, fixing, buttons and beads, and a flower pipe of lavender.

Patted with relic technique of language, land hands crafts and with internet and steep awareness of farming, the fruits of the environment, offer hope like a geyser for us, ourselves, our diversity and curiosity. Our common ground is the shared planet; we gather in living community.

What goes round, goes round

There are a number of ways to get to the centre. Depending on the mode of transport, the paths are many, very many, or a few, very few. Some paths look like they were never finished, as they are less easy to find than others. A few of the paths look like they have been there forever, easy to find and easy to keep to. However, the best paths are not necessarily the ones which are easier to find than others.

In the morning, the texture of the land shows in differences and long views like wooden slats across marsh lands, and other paved roads often touched by stitches that carry distances about them.

During the time between the sun's rise and that bright midday when the eyes see silhouettes, there are paths that show by colour similarities, and these show again during the cooler afternoon before tea.

In the silhouette time of day, the paths are written into the sky, in chimney pots, and the crazy paving of rooftops easy to find in small rural outposts, half drowsing in the distances their diaspora have sung.

After tea, the streets sparkle like Christmas lights, and those lights they put on very tall made things, and on the sky. People can recognise the simpleness of shapes patterning that changing blackness that moves and takes stitches from these things.

Some of the shortest things have the smallest shadows, and these are easy to find from closest to the ground, where the change in the foot and how it places in relation to the knee core-conditions tell the land as it undulates.

In the darkest part of the day, when there is cloud holding the light away from our inquiry, the paths trod are in the general direction which will lead to the middle stitches.

Long term ecology of peatlands and blanket bogs

The peat banks are at the top of the hill, where the peat is thin and close to the rock. They cross the landscape for some distance, each one with a path for an access vehicle, and when it came time to look for more banks to cut, I wandered looking for the best place to cut and carry, with a wheelbarrow and a small car. The further away from the stoney track, the deeper the peats seemed to be, as they are heavier to get to the road.

Close to the road, the land slopes downward and the water runnels grow deeper and deeper, as the wind and water grow small valleys all the way to the bedrock. The white quartz rock shows in the bottom of a rock lake, cupped like the palm of a hand, where the brown-black peat banks are all cut.

Before the turf goes into last year's peat cut, some drainage happens, changing the water flow a little at a time over large areas. Here it is easy to see why restoration of the blanket bog is needed, and why altering the drainage to renew the peatland bog, assists the peat, still growing from the turf.

On the road down from the peats, I could sometimes see the Ness Lighthouse flashing a land warning, speaking at the Western edge of Scotland.

They dug up the Callanish stones from the peat 150 years ago. I have been to the Callanish stones they dug up as they cut the peats. I have travelled there regularly, and I see others who gather on Solstice in summer and some in winter, and a few at the equinox, sharing the awareness of stones put upright by people some 5,000 years ago.

These stones must have seen a sight or two of the people of the ages. Every year there are people there as if standing sentinel.

Seeing the Isles from the top of a peat bank and from the Stones in a sheltered bay, a weigh station for the boats from the north and south, and seeing the Valtos Glen where a great river from the Harris glaciers cut a deep course, seeing time in this land and the people in it. This sustained life, this different life, this edge of Europe's existence, this centre of the shipping routes in times past. This closest edge to America, and somewhere near the middle of democracy, this way of life structures the mind.

The Isles, like reefs catching the Atlantic, shelter the inlands from the sea waves and the weather, changing the pattern with the cutting edge of the land.

Sentinel upon a headland

Sentinel upon a headland
Cutting peat, seeing lights flashing
At houses and distant peaks
Transfer skills; transfer grace.

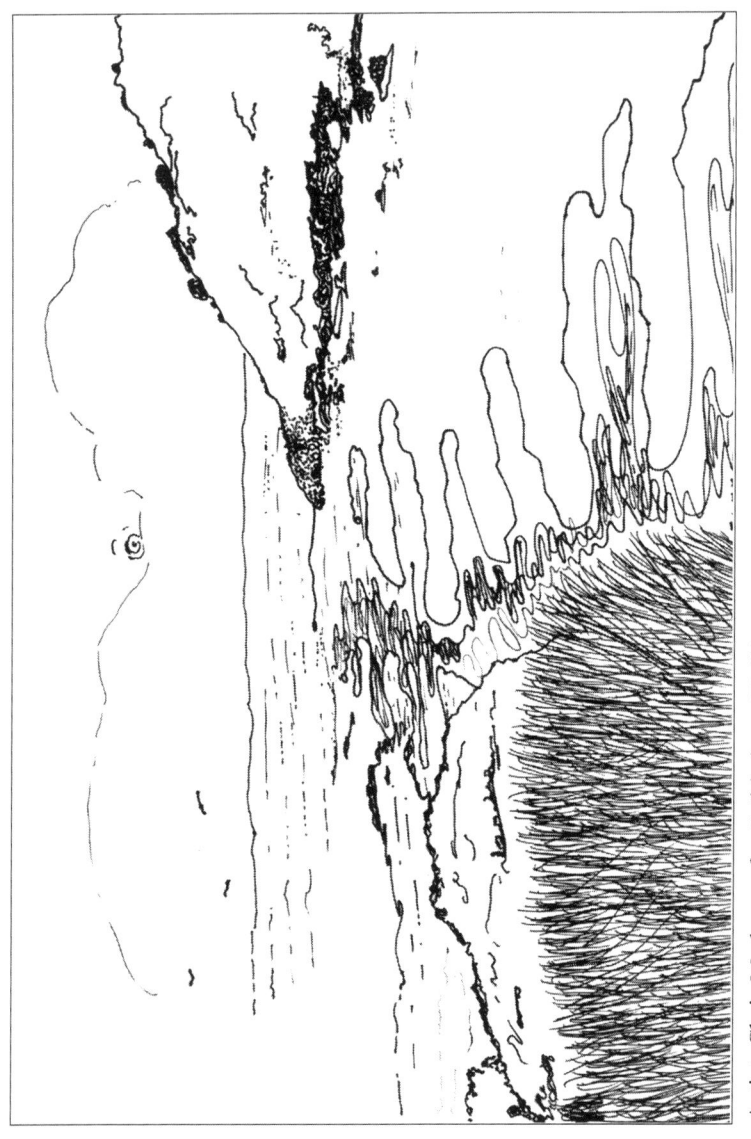

Artist: Chris Matheson for 'Midwinter Walk'

Chris Matheson

Midwinter Walk

The midwinter, northern wind drops
as I emerge out from between
the grass covered sandy hummocks
which protect the foreshore below,
I flail as I flounder to stay upright
on this wet, pebbly, camber,
resting in relief, my tired, bloodshot, gaze
upon the instantly heart-warming
sight of the unspoilt,
a swathe of open sand
outstretched and beckoning

I was alone in this emptiness,
alone, that is, except for the oyster catcher which
emits a hungry cry from out of somewhere invisible,
alone, that is, except for the skein of greylag geese
which emanate in unison a honking call
which faintly echoes as they disappear
through a mist of dusky pink cloud cover,
suspended somewhere
in the middle distance

This place, empty, except for the heave of
the foreboding Paynes-grey sea
as it dashes relentlessly

off the scattered black rocks,
leaving in its wake pools of glistening water which
glint, flashing slivers of cobalt and midnight blue,
the waterlogged sand bathed in the last vestiges
of remaining, radiating, acquiescent, winter sunlight,
shimmers silver as it melts and merges to shadow

I throw my head back in abandon
as I feel every capillary
of my being fill with weightlessness,
as I inhale the cold, salty, air

This is freedom.

Spencer Woodcock

The Tribute of the Chiricahua

The seals, hauled out on their bladderwrack strewn rocks across the bay, raised their heads to gaze back with polite interest. Much nearer, something moved. Alert for otters, Dougie turned and gave a snort.

"The rats are back." He hung his jacket in the porch and went into the living room.

"What?" Melanie did not look up from the sewing machine, but she was smiling.

"Saw one on the foreshore. It must be with the mink eradication." Dougie paused, aware something was up.

"I have some news."

"Cochise killed another rabbit?" This was a joke. Eviscerated wildlife did not make her happy.

"I got some results."

"Results?"

"Results from the doctor."

Dougie stared at his wife.

"You've been to see a doctor? You mean a real doctor?"

A furrow landed lightly on her brow.

"I mean those fans of big pharma in Tarbert."

"But, you're not registered."

"I wasn't. Now I am. It was after what Moira said about social services."

An ache of sudden hope cut through his bemusement.

"These results..?"

Artist: Janine MacDonald for Spencer Woodcock's 'The Tribute of the Chiricahua'

"Yes," her smile widened to a grin, and then it just burst out of her.

"We're going to have a baby."

*

Cochise was a big, big, cat but none of it was fat. He should have scars, Dougie thought, a notched ear or deep scratch on his nose. But Cochise was too formidable for fighting. Cats were few in South Harris, where the holiday home reigned, and none were so stupid as to face him down. Even Murdo-next-door's collies kept a respectful distance.

"Butch," He said one day, "it just came to me."

"Well, you needn't think you're getting leather chaps and one of those Muir caps."

"No, I mean, Butch, the bulldog in Tom and Jerry. How Cochise swaggers."

"I thought that dog was called Spike? Do you want a black-eyed bean? They're organic."

Cochise never mewled, but he could growl, and his purr was like the diesel engine of a distant trawler. He had growled when Dilbert arrived, a great gangling mongrel puppy, already twice his size. Next morning Dougie found the cat ensconced in the dog's new bed, sad-eyed puppy on the cold tile floor, in a posture of submission. He had been unsure what to do, but they sorted it out themselves.

Dilbert, Cochise decreed, could sleep in his own bed in exchange for turning himself into a cosy cat blanket, and certain other duties.

"Melanie, have you seen this?" He had said, aghast.

"What?"

"Dilbert, licking the insides of Cochise's ears out."

"Ugh, gross. Yes, Cochise makes Dilbert clean the bits he can't get at himself. And he has got the poor thing sucking his ticks off."

*

"OK, Yoyo." Dougie pulled the hose out of the hopper on the barge, and swung it back in place. At these moments, he wished that he still smoked, just to have reason to stop and contemplate. The shy Lewis sun, for once, was shining on the jetty. Beyond, rocky islets were scattered in the sea loch. A rusting long-dead winch and scatter of plastic fish boxes in the foreground, salmon cages out in the loch, made the scene fully Hebridean.

"Listen, Calum," he stubbed out his imaginary cigarette.

"Did you have pets when you and Chris-Anne had Tionne?"

"Well, if you can call Idlewild a pet. She's feral really."

"Did she react OK to the baby?"

Calum stopped folding the empty salmon feed bag and considered him.

"Idle was the same as ever, coming in for food when it suited. I've heard of dogs getting jealous, but cats?"

"Aye, I know. It's just...I've been reading up on it. Cats can get upset too if they aren't used to kids. This one woman's cat kept pissing on the baby's things. Its cot, its changing mat. And Cochise is such a brute."

"Reading up on it where?"

"Oh, you know, online."

"Yoyo!" Calum shouted down to the barge. "I can't

take six months of this. We need to find some way to keep this maw off Mumsnet!"

*

A month before the due date, Cochise was banished from the bedroom. Dilbert had long been banned for chewing Melanie's Navajo dreamcatcher to bits. But Cochise, used to going wherever he pleased, was black affronted.

"Will he give up soon, do you think?" Melanie asked.

They lay in bed, listening to insistent scratching. There was a bump, and then another, so heavy that the door visibly juddered.

"Oh, he will hurt himself. Perhaps...?"

Dougie squeezed her hand.

"No. We have to stick with it. Re-set the boundaries before the new arrival. Even Cochise won't be able to train a baby to lick his ear-wax out. At least I hope not."

"I know," she said, as the head-butting continued.

"Though a tick-sucking baby might be useful."

The thumping stopped at last, leaving silence. The house, some way off a quiet road, was very good at silence.

"Should someone go and see?"

She meant should he go, Dougie knew. Melanie had reached the beached whale phase of pregnancy.

"No, no. Leave it. He's probably sitting there in silence, waiting."

They looked at each other.

"You know," said Dougie, "What this situation calls for is some scary music."

Melanie giggled and then stopped, her face creasing with pain. She gripped his hand harder.

"OK?"

"Um... I just had a contraction."

"One of those Braxton Hicks jobs again?"

"Maybe," she winced again. "But better get the rescue remedy and the hospital's number."

*

Amber was a lucky crystal, Melanie said. Dougie managed, somehow, not to point out that it wasn't crystalline. They were both a bit short-tempered with the lack of sleep. He had argued for Angusina; my father has no grandson named for him, he'd pleaded. But only for the joy of seeing his English wife's horrified expression. Amber was a pretty enough name.

And Amber was a very pretty baby. Oh, she shrieked when she was hungry or fractious from lack of sleep. The noise she made seemed to disembowel him; he hated to imagine what it did to Melanie. But when she stopped, unfocussed eyes goggling in bemusement, and when she slept, pink little cheek against the pillow, he thought her the most beautiful thing that he had ever seen. Sometimes he just stood and watched her breathing.

*

"Looks like he's gone for good this time."

Dougie felt a pressure in his chest. He must have become fonder of the old bruiser than he'd realised. Cochise had bristled for days after Amber's arrival, and now he had just vanished.

"No," Melanie looked stricken. "He'll be back. He's just gone for a wander. He's always liked a wander."

She kept talking. Trying to convince herself, he thought, talking away the guilt. She hugged the baby hard to her breasts as if to ease her heartache. Oh, for fuck's sake, thinking of himself as much as Mel. It's just a bloody cat.

"It's well over a week, Melanie. He'll have found himself a cushy berth in Tarbert. Or gone down the Golden Road and caught some camper-vanners."

The old Melanie would have been inconsolable, but this was not that Melanie. This Melanie had a baby, and babies demand feeding, rocking, changing, singing to. And little Amber would have distracted the most distraught cat lover.

*

No seals were to be seen. Dougie rounded the house and heard the sewing machine through an open window.

"Hello, back at work?"

"Yes, I thought I'd make a start. Amber's sleeping, finally."

He smiled. Maybe they would survive this, after all.

"I'll just nip up and check her."

"Don't wake her. I only just now got her down."

Starting up the stairs, a furred blur hurtled past him.

"When did Cochise come back?"

"Cochise? I haven't seen him...Oh, was he upstairs? I left the door open to listen out."

Something ice cold pooled in the bottom of his stomach. Bounding up the stairs, Dougie stepped inside the bedroom. As he looked into the cot, his eyes adjusted to the gloom.

"Oh, fuck..." he whispered to himself. "Oh fuck, Cochise, you monster."

"Dougie! What's happening?"

He stepped out onto the landing, trying to think. He had to stop her from seeing.

"It's all right, mo ghràidh," he called down.

"It's all going to be OK."

He waited until the sewing machine started up again, letting his breathing return to near normal. There was a pile of old Gazettes on the landing. Dougie took a page from the top one. Back in the room, he looked into the cot again; down at the sleeping baby. Next to her little nose, the severed head of a rat, fur rippling in response to the baby's breathing.

Hilary Sludden

After all

It was Friday night. Friends gathered in the least manky cubical of the Ladies', in the bowels of the Corona bar. Titch and Sandra lean over a cracked sink to see their dimly lit reflections, apply clumpy mascara and cherry lip gloss. Our locked cell is a production line. Karen, sideways and to the right of the toilet bowl, has the straightest eye for sticking Rizlas together. She passes her paper art to Melby, who is seated upon the unseated toilet. Melby balances them upon her jeaned knees, adds teased tobacco, sparks her Zippo, and warms our hash to crumb. Professionally, she rolls, placing joints gently in a glasses case for later, for safety. Anne, squeezed in on the left, was chopping speed deftly on the cistern lid.

Our talk is of reading. Titch says she's reading 'The House of Dolls'.

"That's where Joy Division got their name from."

"Watch your bonce Titch," her friends plead.

Titch had been obsessed with war diaries for ages now.

"I know, but it's what happened."

Her attempt to reason is not lost on her friends as they lovingly shake their heavily moussed hair at her.

Karen has just finished 1984. She says it reminds her of her neighbours in a Storwellian Stornoway. It reminds her of gossips, desperate to tell our names and grass up our talk, our behaviours.

Artist: Aaron Watt for Hilary Sludden's 'After All'

"Can I read it next?" Asks Sandra.

"Of course, but there's rats in it?"

"I'll be OK."

"Cosmopolitan has a good article on the pill this month."

"Is that blone in the chemist still looking in the bag when you pick up yours, Sandra?"

"Yes, she's a nosey bitch. The blone in the other chemist is just as bad."

Attired in our best velvet, leather, lace, and denim, we check each other for drug mank. Wired, we sneak out of the pub. We don't want to be banned before being served our first drink, after all.

Bracing ourselves, we headlong it over to the darkest corner of Stornoway's inner harbour. The rain dampening our thighs, we friends run towards our hide, away from the police, away from our parents, away from the leery drunks, swearing at the wind. We huddle, cowering, and attempt to light our spliff.

Titch unearths our carry out from our upturned fish box, alcohol procured earlier after school. She opens a can of lager. We share, we sip and quench our throat trickles. Sandra and Anne talk of the men they'd snogged the night before. They were wishing, willing them to be on the bus to Ness. Titch confesses that she just wishes someone would fancy her.

We share our visions of university places, all together and all separated in the warmth of flats in civilised cities away from our hometown. We sway. We yearn for the concerts we'll go to together. We'll buy better drugs. We sing, quietly and defiantly, trying to include Karen.

Karen's quiet. No Uni for her. She's needed at home, after all.

Clutching our booze, we pick our way towards the parked bus to Ness. Moth-like, we hover by the door, attracted to the light of the warmed bus, and by the chance of a dance in the Ness Hall. Awaiting the driver and glancing at the queue, we scout for new talent. The door opening can't come soon enough.

Macca, the full-of-shit driver, presses his lever; we girls flirt pass him, not paying. Macca allows us on. He always does cos he wants to lay one of us when the doors are locked, and the dance is on. In our pecking orders. We sit. The bears and the older blones at the back, then the randoms and us giggling girls at the front. We pack into seats. We warm with tequila.

Sandra plonks down next to a groomed man, and we speak to him whether he likes it or not. He's nervous. We offer him a slug and a fag, but we're rebuffed. He's not from these shores, after all. Chucking smokes and lighters to each other, we ham it up for this exotic stranger's attention. Groomed-boy's eyes move quickly left, right, and up. We follow his gaze. Long red hair cascades from the luggage rack.

"Anyone seen the Tammie man?" A shout from the back. Anne grabs her chance. It's last night's guy.

"He's crashed out here up in the roof!"

Clambering over Sandra, Groomed-boy runs.

Anne sashays up the hierarchy. Beckoned by a tattooed hand. Sandra follows, making sure her mate is OK, of course. Anne is the youngest, just turned sixteen, after all.

Karen, Melby, and Titch delight in the fact they're left

with their haul, and squeeze in together on a seat to decide on what fag, what can.

We're off! Macca drives into the night, heading north, speeding up towards the moor, and receives his usual heckles.

"Put some decent music on instead of that country shite."

"For fuck's sake! Where did you learn to drive Tarbert?"

"Stop the bus for a piss Macca please."

Macca obliges at his earliest convenience, seizing his chance to leer towards the giggling girls. Long-haired men file past our dilated gazes. The coves line up, backs to the bus, and urinate into the dark.

"Girls piss next."

A mature blone asks for a lookout. Titch is desperate. Grabbing the glasses case and Zippo, she stands and heads for the door. We're not brave enough to add joint smoke to the bus's fug, and envy the dudes at the back because they do. One day.

A biker-jacketed man offers to guard, standing on the bus steps eyeballing Macca. Titch inhales deeply and begins to whitey. Helping her back to her seat, our guardian checks if we are doing ok.

"Wow, he's nice," Melby flashes her best smile as we tuck Titch against the bus wall. He slots into the seat behind.

"I feel sick," Titch moans.

"Oh, fuck Titch, we've got miles to go."

Karen produces a plastic bag, she's a carer, after all.

Not soon enough we reach the village hall, and the

disembarking begins. Nisachs stand outside the hall checking enemies - the Townies, the druggies, the Elvis haters. Titch heads straight on into a ditch, peat covered, she pukes. Melby and Karen hold her handbag and drink. We are soaking in the driving rain.

"Go in," our guardian speaks, giving Macca a warning glance.

"I'll look after her."

What interest does he have in our manky puking friend?

"What's your name cove? Where you from?"

"I'm Murdo from Gravir. I'll make sure she's OK. What's her name?"

"It's Titch."

Titch indicates she'll be OK.

"We'll get you inside," Murdo reassures.

Melby takes the huff.

"How can he fancy her in that state?"

"Admired her from afar?"

Sandra, Anne, Melby, and Karen re-group in the bogs for safety. A fight has broken out between the boy racers and Elvis fans.

Knock knock on the door.

"Engaged!"

"It's Murdo from the bus. Titch is here and her nose is bleeding, but she's not sick anymore."

Embracing their amigo, they search handbags for tissues.

"Titch, do you work Saturdays?" Murdo asks.

"The Coffee Pot café," Melby whispers, getting up close to Murdo.

"I'll call in the affa, Titch."

Titch says she can't wait, Karen replies on her behalf. Melby can't believe her peat-stained, puking and bloody friend has scored.

The band strikes Free Bird. Hurdling the punks doing the Dead Fly, clutching each other, we make a raft, a life raft against our waves of adversity, our journeys unknown. We sway and sing with unclipping wings. We rock it out, back to the bus.

Macca's giggling catch is perched on the dashboard. It was four in the morning and moods are mellowing. Work tomorrow, final exams on Monday after all.

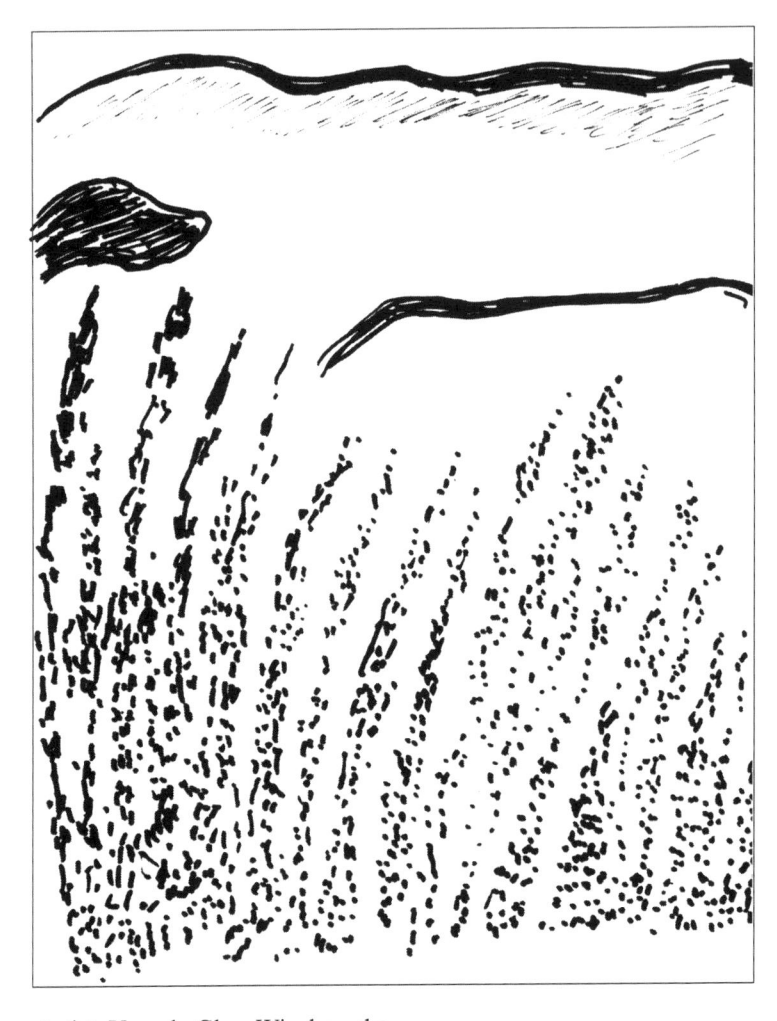

Artist: Urszula Ghee Wieckowska

Urszula Ghee Wieckowska

Island Life in May

Travelling along the road,
on a sunny May afternoon,
I see the sea on both sides,
also, there are bushes of gorse,
deep yellow, golden yellow,
and patches of bluebells,
the heather brown,
not yet in flower

The big skies above,
blue but with some clouds,
clouds floating, fluffy white,
with some grey,
the sun bright and warm

But then there are alternate days,
grey, dull, and misty,
but still the big skies,
and the birds still fly

Longer and longer days,
the sun staying out later,
then it can rain heavily,
the weather can change,

the mist can come,
the mornings are often misty

Late May, the rhododendron bushes flower,
lots of pink and purple
add to the general colours,
and the grass is now bright green,
so May is my favourite month of colour.

A Walking Meditation

We walk towards St Columba's Church,
along the great expanse of sand,
and rest upon the solitary rock,
beneath the roofless walls,
grass growing along their tops,
water lapping gently on the shore

Then we walk up to the ruined church,
and learn that it is called
Eaglais na h-Aoidhe - The Eye Church,
built in late fourteenth century times
but it is generally accepted that Catan,
another, early, Irish saint,
established a cell on the site at Uidh

The cult of Columba grew in Scotland
in the Middle Ages,
and many churches of that period,
like St Columba's at Uidh,
were dedicated to the saint.

And Catan in his cell lived here,
in sixth-century time,
and also sat looking at the sea,
praying, fasting, I surmise

We go back to shelter warm
Take something from this place
Knowing that we will come again.

Artist Urszula Ghee Wieckowska for her poem 'A Walking Meditation'

Cemeteries

Whenever I can, I visit the cemetery,
every day I pass it on my way,
I know where our grave is located
he is already in it,
'We are made of star dust,'
'Rest and be thankful'

I remember the day he was interred,
he came back from Inverness,
our friends and family carried his coffin
through the cemetery to the open grave

I did not want to throw soil onto his coffin,
so I threw a yellow rose,
but it was a windy day and
the wind kept blowing it out,
a friendly undertaker finally
picked up that rose
and placed it on the coffin

He was not a religious man,
the chaplain read out a poem I had written,
then we went to our favourite cafe,
we all sat upstairs and shared
a meal and stories

Cemeteries here on the island
are usually by the sea,
so I visit and sit on the granite bench

I had erected instead of a headstone,
and watch the sea lapping and
look at the hills

The sky is a lovely colour
when the sun is setting

I sit and feel close to him,
waiting for when my time comes
and I can join him
on this beautiful Hebridean island.

My Island Home

We came to the island
to look for a new home,
now that we were both retired,
our caring duties
were no longer needed

We travelled the width and length
of the island
looking at all the available properties,
but some homes never come up for sale
as they are left within families

We found a house in Point,
on a large plot of land called a croft,
facing the sea at the back,
and the sea at the front, and with
a lovely large garden round the house

We went back to Nottingham
to oversee the sale of our own house,
and eventually, we packed up
and arranged to move up

We used to have a car,
so we discovered the shops and beaches,
found our way around,
discovering hidden gems

We acquired a flock of ducks,
three females and four males,
and looked after them,
fed them poultry corn.

The females laid eggs
larger than chicken eggs,
occasionally they hatched,
we saw the little ducklings
running round looking very cute

Next door's chickens and cockerels
came round to visit,
lots of sheep and lambs in the
surrounding fields, gambolling,
crows sat and watched out
for left over food.

Sometimes, a buzzard comes
and sits on the fence,
observing the ducklings
which the ducks look after,
protecting and hiding them
under bushes, and we hear t
the cuckoo sing its song,
so, lots to see and hear
in our island home.

Basking Sharks

It was a typical shopping day,
we were driving home and on the Braighe
we noticed disturbances in the sea,
we stopped and looked,
there they were,
a school of basking sharks
circling round and round,
they each were so long
I saw a head and then moved my head
to the side and eventually saw the tail,
their bodies circled round
making huge circumferences,
and we stayed and watched them
circling, swimming,
their open jaws
scooping the plankton,
I saw the open mouth
and eventually the tail
so big but quite harmless to us

We stood and watched and marvelled
at this wonder of nature.

Artist: Zoe Digges for Ozrik Carter's 'Island Life'

Ozrik Carter

Island Life

I came to Stornoway from Nottingham, and I have been on the Isle of Lewis since I was nine years old. I am 30 now, and the island has always been a home to me, with beautiful landscapes, wild life included.

I feel very fortunate to feel accepted here, and enjoy and appreciate island life. It truly is a beautiful place with beautiful people and lovely locations to explore.

Every day, you see different birds in the sky. As I feed the wildlife, I am uncertain what I might see as time goes on. Every day, we might at least look to the sky, or at something beautiful and different that's wild.

We are individuals, created as individuals with our own nature, temperament, and creativity. Island life isn't just about whether we are born on the island, but learning what the difference between us and the island is.

Island life is interesting in a positive manner, and full of surprises - like a box of chocolates, you never know what to expect from one instance to the next. I guess we sum it up in a nutshell - 'the blue yonder.'

What we are, and what we do, is sealed by our own minds, our own luck. But, however, we always put a question mark - the what ifs, when's, where's, and hows. We alone are individuals of our own creations, all wonderfully made.

Island life isn't just about if we live here or not. It's a

unique place. We should not be so discreet with mainlanders, but show them the culture and teachings, and be welcoming, as if we were sitting next to them, or if they were our fellow neighbours, and vice versa.

Printed in Great Britain
by Amazon